FLUTTERBY FLY

Written by Stephen Cosgrove
Illustrated by Robin James

A Serendipity™ *Book*

PRICE STERN SLOAN
Los Angeles

Dedicated to the memory of the real Flutterby. She died too soon ever to be able to fly.

Stephen

Beyond the farthest mountain, in a place where the feathery wisps of mist begin to call themselves clouds, there is a long winding valley called Wingsong. The lush trees of the valley seemed to dance with blossoms and the leaves seemed to flutter in the gentle breezes that sighed as they reached up and touched the sky.

The trees appeared to lose all their leaves as a breeze wrapped itself around the rocks and trees alike and then lifted itself toward the warming sun. But appearances can be deceiving, for the leaves were really butterflies, millions and millions of butterflies that flittered and fluttered about the valley in search of memories of a long lost time.

For it was here in the valley of Wingsong that all the butterflies we chased when we were young came when summer's warmth turned to winter's cold.

They flew to Wingsong on gentle fall breezes and then gathered together in flights of a hundred or more. Once in Wingsong they were, forevermore, softly herded from one spot to the next by small winged horses. The tiny horses would flap their wings faster than a hummingbird and swiftly fly from one end of a flight of butterflies to the other to ensure that no one got lost.

One such small, winged horse was named Flutterby and oh, how she could fly! She would dip and soar on the smallest of breezes, watching for one laughing butterfly who would try to flap away from the flight on a tiny giggle of wind.

As one would try to slip away, to who knows what adventure, Flutterby, with a kick of her crystal heels, would swoop quickly around and guide the silly butterfly back to its own flight.

One day, as Flutterby was guiding her flight through a grove of clover rose, she began to hear the butterflies whispering to one another. The whispering got louder and louder and all of their wings started beating against the rhythm of the winds. One minute the butterflies were in organized flight, a giant puff of shimmering color floating through the air; the next minute, they were flying in a hundred different directions. It was like a rainbow's explosion as they went this way and that.

Flutterby flew as she was trained, around and around, whinnying soft and gentle sounds to the butterflies as they began to slow down.

When the flight was calm and together again Flutterby flew to the point and asked the butterflies, "Why? Why did you suddenly fly all over the sky?"

The butterflies were still a bit skitterish but finally one of them answered, "Because of the words that we heard dancing on the wind!"

Flutterby couldn't believe that a few words could cause such a panic. "What words?" she asked patiently.

"Well," one of the butterflies said in a gossipy tone, "This is what we heard: 'Ugly, ugly butterfly. Fly away or you shall die!' "

Flutterby reared back in shock. "Who would say such a thing?"

The butterfly paused and then said, "I shouldn't tell you, for it was a secret, but . . . it was the old black raven that flies in the wood."

Flutterby settled her butterflies on a lilac bush and then went off in search of the old black raven that flies in the wood. She didn't have to go far, for within a hundred beats of her wings she found the old, black raven sitting in a cherry tree, spitting pits. Flutterby was furious but she held her temper and through clenched jaws said, "Did you tell the butterflies: 'Ugly, ugly butterfly. Fly away or you shall die?' "

"No!" cawed the raven, "They must have misunderstood me, or perhaps the wind took away part of the words. I told the butterflies exactly what I had heard: 'Don't sigh, butterfly. Fly away or you shall cry!' "

"Who would say such a thing?" Flutterby asked.

"Well," crowed the raven in a gossipy whisper, "It was a secret and I promised not to tell, but it was that chubby chipmunk that lives in the tall oak tree that grows at the edge of the woods."

Flutterby fluttered her wings in anger and then flew just as fast as she could to the tall oak tree the raven had described.

She soared high above the tree and flew around and around until she spied the chipmunk sitting on his haunches at the end of a branch. It was chattering away just as loud as it could please to anyone and everyone who would listen.

Flutterby fluttered down and in a stern voice asked, "Are you the gossipy chipmunk who told the raven: 'Don't sigh, butterfly. Fly away or you shall cry!' and then the raven told the butterflies: 'Ugly, ugly butterfly. Fly away or you shall die!' "

"Heavens to betsy, no!" chattered the chipmunk. "I don't know how that raven misunderstood me because I told him exactly what I had heard: 'Better fly, butterfly. Fly away and don't you lie.' "

"Who would say such a thing?" asked Flutterby.

"Well," said the chipmunk in a conspiratorial tone, "I wasn't going to tell anybody, but . . . it was the old monarch butterfly that lives at the base of this very tree."

Flutterby snorted, stomped her foot in anger and then stepped off the branch and flew around and around the tree until she came to a gnarled branch nearly at the base. There, sitting in a shaft of golden sunlight, was an ancient monarch butterfly waving his tattered wings against a warm summer breeze.

Flutterby landed and after scraping her hooves against the bark of the tree asked, "Are you the butterfly that told the chipmunk: 'Better fly, butterfly. Fly away and don't you lie!' The chipmunk who told the raven: 'Don't sigh, butterfly. Fly away or you shall cry!' The raven who told the butterflies: 'Ugly, ugly butterfly. Fly away or you shall die!' "

The old butterfly flapped his wings and twisted his antenna this way and that, tasting the light and gentle breeze. "Not I," he said in a deep, rich voice, "but I do speak to all the new, young butterflies that come to Wingsong. As they touch their very first scented wind I always tell them: 'Fly so high, little butterfly. Fly away and touch the sky!' "

"Gossips!" snorted Flutterby, as she thanked the old butterfly and went back to her flight at the end of the valley.

She circled the flight and finally went to the very center and said, "Listen, little butterflies. There is nothing to fear. What you heard before was only gossip, only lies!"

All of the butterflies nodded their antennae in simple understanding as Flutterby guided them once again on the wings of their journey. But far, far in the back of the pack voices could be heard:

"What did she say?"

"I couldn't hear that well. Something about worship and sighs."

"What did you say?"

"I heard the same thing," said another in a gossipy tone. "Flutterby was beat with a horsewhip and nearly died!"

If you want to gossip
and it's an easy thing to do
Gossip to a butterfly
The story will come out untrue!

Serendipity™ Books

Created by
Stephen Cosgrove and Robin James

Enjoy all the delightful books in the Serendipity™ Series:

The above books, and many others, can be bought wherever books are sold.

PRICE STERN SLOAN
Los Angeles